# Megan
## and the
# Night
# Diamond

# Collect all six Arctica Mermaid books

# Also look out for the six original Mermaid SOS adventures in Coral Kingdom

# Megan
## and the
# Night
# Diamond

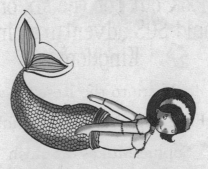

## gillian shields

### illustrated by helen Turner

BLOOMSBURY
CHILDREN'S
BOOKS

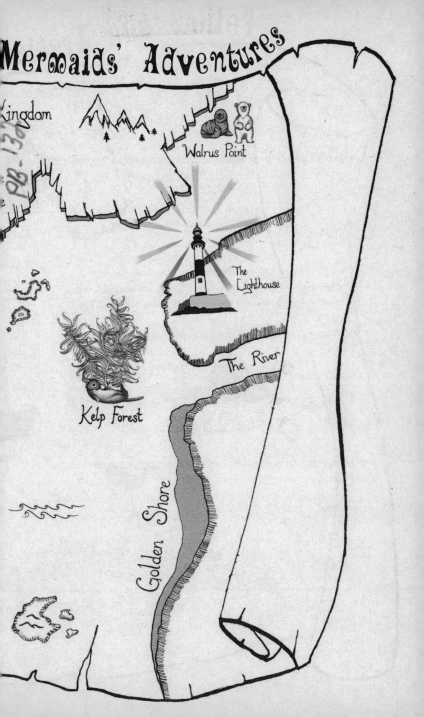

First published in Great Britain in 2007 by Bloomsbury Publishing Plc,
36 Soho Square, London, W1D 3QY

Text copyright © 2007 by Gillian Shields
Illustrations copyright © 2007 by Helen Turner

A CIP catalogue record of this book is available from the British Library

ISBN 978 0 7475 8970 9

Printed and bound in Great Britain by Clays Ltd, St Ives Plc

1 3 5 7 9 10 8 6 4 2

All papers used by Bloomsbury Publishing are natural, recyclable products
made from wood grown in well-managed forests. The manufacturing processes
conform to the environmental regulations of the country of origin.

For Lottie

*– G.S.*

For the St. Thomas More Girls –
Jo Len, Jo Lee, Lisa, Debs
and Kathryn

*– Love H.T.*

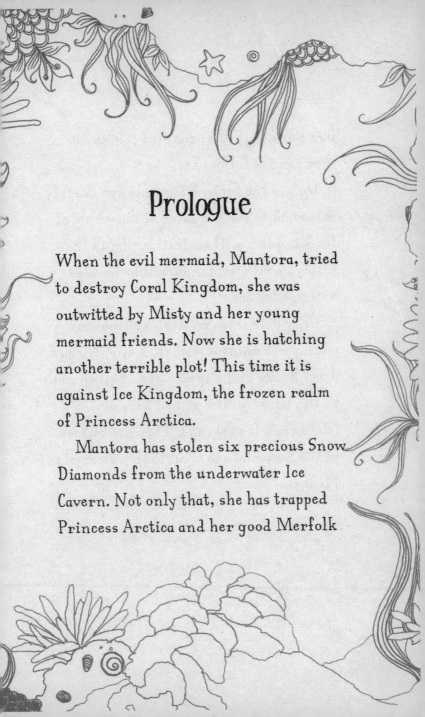

# Prologue

When the evil mermaid, Mantora, tried
to destroy Coral Kingdom, she was
outwitted by Misty and her young
mermaid friends. Now she is hatching
another terrible plot! This time it is
against Ice Kingdom, the frozen realm
of Princess Arctica.

Mantora has stolen six precious Snow
Diamonds from the underwater Ice
Cavern. Not only that, she has trapped
Princess Arctica and her good Merfolk

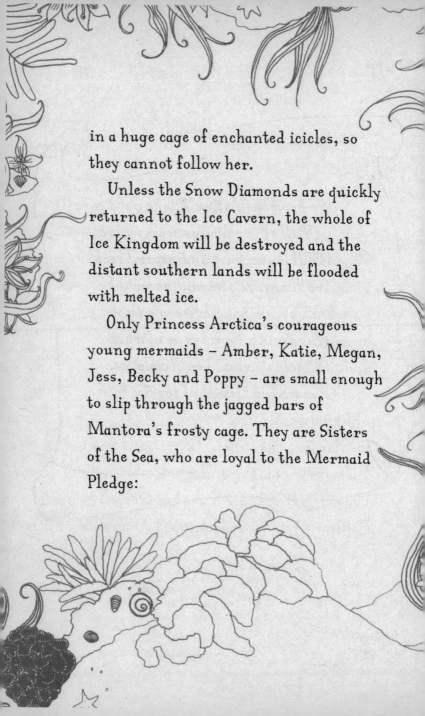

in a huge cage of enchanted icicles, so they cannot follow her.

Unless the Snow Diamonds are quickly returned to the Ice Cavern, the whole of Ice Kingdom will be destroyed and the distant southern lands will be flooded with melted ice.

Only Princess Arctica's courageous young mermaids – Amber, Katie, Megan, Jess, Becky and Poppy – are small enough to slip through the jagged bars of Mantora's frosty cage. They are Sisters of the Sea, who are loyal to the Mermaid Pledge:

We promise that we'll take good care
Of all sea creatures everywhere.
We'll never hurt and never break,
We'll always give and never take.
And as we fight Mantora's threat,
This saying we must not forget:
'I'll help you and you'll help me,
For we are Sisters of the Sea!'

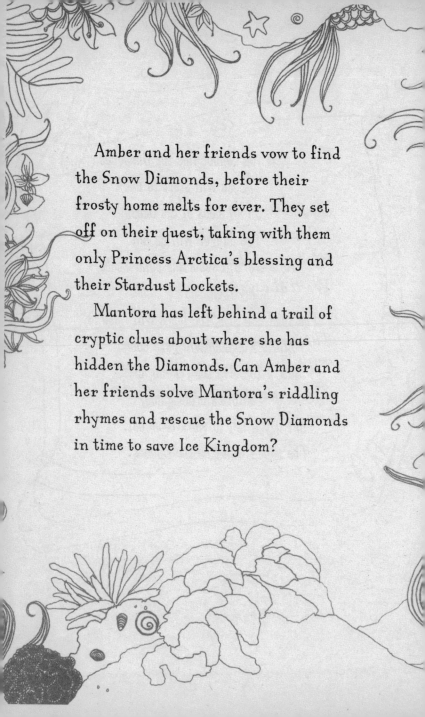

Amber and her friends vow to find the Snow Diamonds, before their frosty home melts for ever. They set off on their quest, taking with them only Princess Arctica's blessing and their Stardust Lockets.

Mantora has left behind a trail of cryptic clues about where she has hidden the Diamonds. Can Amber and her friends solve Mantora's riddling rhymes and rescue the Snow Diamonds in time to save Ice Kingdom?

If you cannot find the Diamonds,
The ice will start to melt.
On all sides of the Ocean,
The danger will be felt.
No more will seals and polar bears
Enjoy their snowy home,
The seas will rise, the lands will flood –
Storm Kingdom will have come!
So try to solve the riddling clues
Of Mantora's cruel game,
But if you fail to work them out,
The world won't be the same ...

Megan

# Chapter One

Megan and her mermaid friends – Amber, Katie, Jess, Becky and Poppy – were sitting on the snowy headland at Walrus Point. They tucked their sparkling tails underneath them, as they crowded around a small, blood-red scroll. It contained a message from Mantora, who had stolen the six precious Snow Diamonds.

'Do read it to us quickly, Megan,' said

her friends anxiously. They had already found the first two Snow Diamonds, which were now hidden safely in Amber and Katie's magical Stardust Lockets. But the young mermaids still had four more Lockets to fill before they could save Ice Kingdom from being destroyed.

Megan unrolled the scroll, her fingers

trembling slightly, and began to read
Mantora's riddling rhyme aloud:

Diamond bright,

Diamond light,

Diamond shining

In the night,

By the distant golden shore,

Ever less and ever more!

As she finished reading, Megan looked up
at the other mermaids. They were all
sitting open-mouthed in stunned silence.

'Something that is *"ever less and ever
more"*?' groaned Poppy. 'But that's just not
possible. Mantora's gone too far this time!'

'Wait,' said Amber. 'There's a second
note from Mantora, tucked inside the

scroll.' She picked up another piece of crimson parchment and quickly read out the message:

'So, now you have two Diamonds – but that will not help you to save Ice Kingdom. Only if you return all six Diamonds to the Ice Cavern will the world be safe. And that, my not-so-dear little mermaids is like this clue – IMPOSSIBLE.
How I shall laugh, watching your feeble attempts to work out my best riddle yet. What fun this will be – for me!'

'We've got to prove her wrong,' added Amber determinedly. 'This clue might look impossible, but surely we can think of something that will help to unravel it?'

Megan looked round at her friends. 'I'm not sure if this will help,' she said uncertainly, 'but do you remember the old

Mermaid song about the Golden Shore?'

She shyly hummed a quick tune and the other mermaids soon joined in, singing sweetly:

*'Golden Shore,*
*In the South,*
*By the flowing*
*River's mouth,*
*Where the otters*
*Swim and play,*
*In the long*
*And golden day.'*

'I've often played that tune on my Mermaid Harp,' said Katie, who was very musical. 'But I thought the Golden Shore in the south was only a legend?'

'Many truths are hidden in old legends and stories,' said Becky, wisely nodding her sleek, dark head.

'Then perhaps the third Diamond really is hidden in the distant Southern seas,' replied Megan. 'Do you think we could travel so far from Ice Kingdom?'

'We don't have any choice,' said Poppy. 'Princess Arctica needs us to get those Diamonds back – and fast!'

'Monty will take us there as quickly as he can,' added Jess. 'So, is it agreed?'

Monty was a friendly humpback whale. He had offered to speed the mermaids to

wherever they needed to go in their search for the Diamonds. Megan and the others nodded solemnly in reply, 'Agreed!'

The next part of their quest was now clear. The mermaids had to leave their frozen home in Ice Kingdom far behind, and go to strange new lands in the sunny south.

Megan whispered to her pet, 'Are you coming with us, Sammy?'

A tiny Fairy Shrimp poked his head out of Megan's furry pocket and waggled his feelers.

'Of course I am,' squeaked Sammy bravely. 'You'll need me to look after you!'

With a flick of her pink and white spangled tail, Megan dived from the ice into the clear green waves. Her friends followed her like a shower of coloured raindrops. They all swept along, racing to find Monty, with courageous hearts and smiling faces.

But as the mermaids darted through the cold sea, Megan secretly couldn't help feeling a little nervous. She knew that there would be danger lurking wherever Mantora's trail of teasing clues led them. What would happen to them next, in the quest for the third Snow Diamond? There

was only one way to find out, and that
was to head for the mysterious Golden
Shore…

After what seemed a long, long time,
Megan asked, 'Are we there yet, Monty?'

The huge humpback whale was gliding
swiftly through the underwater deeps of
the warm, wide ocean. The Sisters of the

Sea had travelled far from Ice Kingdom, holding tightly to Monty's broad back.

'Don't worry, we'll soon be there,' said Monty cheerfully. 'We humpback whales swim to the Golden Shore every year, when Ice Kingdom becomes too cold for us. I know the way very well. But would you like me to rise to the surface and check where we are?'

'Oh, yes please, Monty,' said the mermaids eagerly. Even though they knew that their quest was very urgent and serious, it was still exciting to see new lands and seas.

'Hold on tight to the Whale Express!' cried Monty. His strong, sleek body raced upwards, swooshing silver bubbles through the water. Megan and her friends clung on determinedly, their shining hair streaming out like silk. Suddenly, Monty leapt out of the sea with a huge thrust of his powerful tail. For a moment he seemed to fly through the air, then he plunged back under the waves, like an enormous rollercoaster.

'Ooooh!' shouted the mermaids in delight, tumbling off into the clear blue sea, as Monty sank deep under the water. The young friends bobbed up and down in the waves, swishing their glistening tails and enjoying the warm sunshine. Then

Megan checked that Sammy wasn't too shaken up after Monty's acrobatic leap.

'Are you all right, Sammy?' she said. He was sitting on her shoulder, and looking around.

'That was like flying,' chirped Sammy, giving his dainty feelers a shake. 'But where are we?'

'We're much further south, that's for sure,' replied Megan, cuddling him softly, then gazing at the bright sky. 'It's really hot here!'

'We don't need all our warm clothes now,' said Amber. The others agreed. Megan quickly took off her furry jacket and smoothed down her soft wavy hair. Soon, all the mermaids were just wearing their little sparkly tops, decorated with shells and stars and snowflakes.

'Phew! I feel better now,' said Jess. 'But

Sammy's got a good point – where are we?'

'It doesn't look anything like Ice Kingdom,' replied Katie, her eyes growing big with wonder. 'Look at that long sandy coastline in the distance. It looks like a ribbon of gold, glinting in the sun.'

'That must be the Golden Shore,' said Megan, in an awestruck voice. 'We've made it!'

# Chapter Two

'We certainly have,' boomed Monty, raising his huge head above the water. 'The bright shoreline over there is where you need to start your search, where the river meets the sea.'

Across the waves, the mermaids could see the wide mouth of a river flowing into a curved bay. On one side of the bay, a tall white lighthouse stood on some rocks.

'Perhaps we could ask the creatures who live in these blue waters to help us,' said Becky dreamily. She loved everything beautiful, and was thrilled by the colours of the mild sea, and the brilliance of the golden sun. It was so very different from the frozen world of Ice Kingdom.

'Let's start straight away,' said Amber. 'I vote that we leave our warm clothes here and swim to the shore. Then we can start looking for the Diamond.'

The others agreed that this was a good plan. They rolled their thick jackets up

33

and tied them together with a furry scarf.
Then they let the bundle drop safely on to
the ocean bed, ready to be collected again
later.

'Goodbye for the moment, dear Monty,'
said Megan. 'Please wait here for us and
wish us luck!'

She planted a kiss on the friendly
whale's nose, and tucked Sammy safely

into her sparkly
belt. Her pink
and white tail
shimmered as
she started to
swim towards
the sunny coast.
Megan's friends
darted after

her, like a cluster of brilliant butterflies.
As the mermaids swam swiftly side by
side, they thought about the important
task that lay ahead of them.

'I'm sure the "*Diamond in the night*"
must be a star, like my Stardust Locket,'
said Poppy confidently, as she shook her
coppery curls out of her eyes. 'What does
everyone else think?'

But nobody got the chance to answer
her. At that moment, a flock of black birds
suddenly flew overhead, screeching fiercely.

'Storm Gulls!' shouted Jess.

Megan looked up in horror. These cruel,
cunning birds were the servants of Mantora.

In one wild swoop, the Storm Gulls
dived to attack the mermaids with their
curved beaks, blocking the way to the

yellow sands with their ragged wings.

'Shoo! Oh, go away, you horrid things,' exclaimed Katie. The mermaids did their best to drive the Gulls away by wildly waving their arms and flapping their hands about. As they did so, Megan noticed something. The Storm Gulls were only attacking Amber and Katie, pecking greedily at the silver bracelets where their delicate Stardust Lockets hung.

'Katie! Amber!' she gasped. 'Be careful – the Storm Gulls are trying to snatch your Lockets!'

'Megan's right,' cried Poppy, as the fierce birds crowded round Amber and Katie. 'Look out!'

'Dive down, everyone, as quickly as you can!' shouted Jess.

Megan and her friends instantly dived under the warm blue waves. Then they hovered underwater, holding hands and clinging on to one another. Up above, they could see that the Storm Gulls were still skimming over the surface of the sea.

'Oh, what a fright,' said Megan. 'Are the Diamonds still safe after that attack?'

Katie and Amber hurriedly opened their gleaming Stardust Lockets. Katie's was shaped like a leaping fish and Amber's like a soaring sea bird. The friends breathed a sigh of relief. Both of the Snow Diamonds glittered like living ice, nestled safely in their magical Lockets.

'Thank goodness they're not damaged,' said Megan, 'You did well to stop the Storm Gulls snatching them.'

'But why were they trying to grab them?' asked Becky, frowning over the birds' strange behaviour.

'Because they are mean and nasty?' suggested Poppy, rubbing a big bruise on her arm where she had been pecked.

'I think it must be more than that,' replied Megan. 'Mantora seemed so sure that we wouldn't even solve the first clue, and yet here we are right next to the Golden Shore, where the third Diamond is hidden. Perhaps she is worried that we really will manage to find all six of them, and spoil her wicked plans?'

'And so she's trying to steal them back!

Well, she won't succeed,' said Jess, flicking her turquoise tail impatiently.

'But how can we get past the Storm Gulls?' asked Megan, with a worried face. 'The clue said that the Diamond is by the shore, not under the waves. But if we go up to the surface the Gulls will attack us.'

'We certainly won't find the Diamond stuck underwater, hiding down here from the Storm Gulls,' declared Poppy. 'We've *got* to get past them to the shore somehow.'

The little mermaids weren't quite sure what to do, though they were determined not to let the Gulls ruin their quest.

'Perhaps they will have given up and gone by now,' said Becky hopefully. 'Come on, let's try again.'

But this time it was even worse. The Storm Gulls were waiting as the mermaids peered over the waves, ready to grab and tear and rip and snatch.

'OOOH!' yelped Katie and Amber, as the birds pecked them fiercely and tried to steal the Stardust Lockets from their wrists.

'It's no good,' panted Megan. 'The Gulls are too strong for us. Dive! Dive! Follow me!'

# Chapter Three

The mermaids swam urgently, down, down, down through the blue water, racing swiftly after Megan. They hardly saw where they were heading, as they dashed away from the dangerous birds.

Megan kept peering over her shoulder to check that no other evil creatures were nearby. She knew that Mantora had whole armies of poisonous jellyfish. Perhaps they were lurking near too, ready to attack the mermaids at any moment…

'Be careful, everyone,' she called, looking back to make sure that her friends were safe. But just as she called out, Megan found herself suddenly floundering in the deep water. Without noticing where she was going, the brave young mermaid had swum into a tangle of long strands of seaweed.

'Oh!' she spluttered. 'I'm all tied up!'

'Help!' squeaked Sammy, from where he clung to Megan's sparkly belt.

The others quickly streamed forward to help Megan and her pet. Becky's nimble fingers soon untangled her friend from the thick fronds.

'Thank you,' said Megan, slightly out of breath. 'That was silly of me. I didn't look where I was going.' Then she gazed wonderingly at the tall, waving clumps that were growing up from the sea bed.

'We've reached the edge of a kelp forest,' Katie exclaimed. With a ripple of her pale lemon-coloured tail, she started to swim through the swaying groves. The others followed her, twisting in and out of the ribbons of purple kelp.

'This would be a great place to hide,' said Becky, peeping down the thick avenues of seaweed trees.

'If only we could hide from the Storm Gulls somehow,' added Jess.

'We'd need to do more than hide to get past those mean things,' muttered Poppy.

'We'd need to be invisible – and that really is impossible!'

Megan suddenly swirled round in the water and came to a halt in a flurry of silver bubbles. Her brown eyes gleamed as an idea popped into her head.

'Perhaps that isn't as impossible as it sounds,' she said. 'Don't you remember what Princess Arctica said? She told us that the Stardust Lockets would help us, "*in more ways than you can imagine*".'

The friends gathered round Megan, hovering between the waving fronds of kelp.

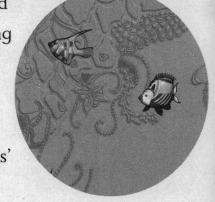

'Do you really think that the Lockets' magical powers

could make us invisible, Megan?' they murmured.

'There's only one way to find out,' said Megan. She gracefully raised her arm in the clear water. The heart-shaped Locket on her bracelet twinkled like a bright star. Her friends did the same, lifting their arms high above their heads, as if they were doing a Mermaid Dance.

The Stardust Lockets glittered brightly. Each Locket was a miniature version of the marvellous carved statues in the Ice Cavern back home. As well as Megan's heart there was a fish, a bird, a dolphin, a flowery anemone and a star. The light of the great North Star had been captured in the Lockets, and they shone with magical radiance.

Softly, the mermaids sang together:

'*Stardust Lockets, please hear us now,*
*Help us trick our enemies somehow.*
*Hide us from the Storm Gulls' sight,*
*Dazzle them with your magical light!*'

Then they held their breaths, waiting to
see if anything wonderful would happen.

Suddenly, the Lockets began to spin on
the mermaids' bracelets, making a low

humming sound. A shower of silver sprinkles burst from each one of the shining Lockets, and fell around the young friends. The sprinkles dissolved to form a strange, transparent cloud. The cloud wrapped itself round the mermaids like a silvery-blue mist.

'I think it's working,' cried Megan. 'You all look hazy round the edges.'

'Let's find out whether the Gulls can still see us,' said Poppy boldly. 'Ready? Follow me!'

Megan and the others swam swiftly up to the surface through the long strands of kelp. The magical mist still clung to them. Silently and carefully, the mermaids lifted their heads above the waves.

As they did so, they saw the Storm Gulls

skimming over the water, searching for them. But the snooping, snapping birds didn't seem to notice the mermaids. The young friends were hidden from their enemies' eyes by the silvery cloud. They really were invisible!

'The Sisters of the Sea have gone,' croaked the leader of the Gulls. 'They have slipped past us somehow. Fly back at once

to the far horizon and search for them there. The birds wheeled round in formation and streaked away like black arrows, heading out of sight.

'Hooray!' exclaimed the mermaids, when

the Storm Gulls had finally gone. 'We fooled them. They can't snatch the Diamonds back now.'

'And we can start looking for the third one without being attacked again,' said Megan happily. The strange pearly cloud floated away from the mermaids, up into the clear sky, then disappeared in a shimmer of silver sprinkles.

'That was amazing,' said Amber in astonishment. 'Those Gulls really couldn't see us.'

'No, they couldn't,' said a friendly voice beside them. 'But I can!'

The mermaids swirled round in the sparkling waves. A furry creature with twinkling eyes and a pointed black nose was watching them curiously. He was

floating on his back, and studying them
with an amused expression.

'Otto the Sea Otter at your service,' he
said, with a flourish of his paw. 'And why
would six young Sisters of the Sea need to
make themselves
invisible in a magic
cloud?'

Megan and the others quickly told him all about Mantora, the stolen Snow Diamonds, and their quest to solve the third clue. As Otto listened carefully, his expression changed. He looked serious, even gloomy, as he clutched his paws together over his furry chest.

'Ah,' he sighed. 'So many strange things are happening to our seas. The waters are warming, the seasons are changing, and our life is harder than it used to be. The Humans are too busy with their factories and fumes to notice what is happening to us sea creatures. But if Mantora destroys Ice Kingdom, what will become of the world?'

'Don't worry, Otto,' said the mermaids. 'We're going to stop her by getting all the Diamonds back. We promised Princess

Arctica that we would.'

'But we're just not sure where to start with this part of our task,' added Megan, with an anxious expression. 'This is such a difficult clue.'

'Perhaps things will become clearer when the sun sets,' replied Otto wisely. 'Didn't you say the clue was about a *"Diamond shining in the night…"*?'

'Yes,' interrupted Poppy, with a confident air. 'I'm sure that means something to do with the stars.'

'Then why not rest in our beautiful kelp forest until the stars come out?' suggested Otto, suddenly twisting himself round playfully in the water. 'Then you can visit our Golden Shore by starlight, and hopefully find what you are looking for.'

Megan and her friends looked at one another. It seemed like a good idea to rest for a while, after the fright they'd had with the Storm Gulls.

'We'd love to,' they chorused. 'But we must get back to work as soon as the night falls.'

'Excellent!' grinned Otto. 'Now come and meet my family.'

# Chapter Four

'This is my wife, Ottilie,' said Otto
proudly. 'And this is my daughter, Lottie.'

Otto and Ottilie floated happily on their
backs, as they watched their little
daughter say hello to each mermaid in
turn. Lottie had thick, fluffy fur and bright
eyes that were full of fun.

'Let's play hide and seek,' she chattered.
'It's my favourite game!'

Soon, Megan and the others were darting through the water in a wild game with the sea otters; hiding in the dense groves of kelp, then twisting and turning as they raced for 'home'. Lottie squealed with excitement as she played with her new friends. But when they were all tired and out of breath, Ottilie gently caught her little daughter in her furry arms.

'Time for bed, Lottie,' she said, carrying her back to the surface. 'The stars are coming out.'

Megan looked up at the wide, clear sky. The sun was setting over the ocean. A scattering of stars was beginning to glimmer above the mermaids. A few elegant seabirds, called shearwaters, flew gracefully overhead.

'I hadn't noticed the time passing,' Megan murmured. 'It was like being at home before our quest began, just playing with Lottie and not worrying about anything.'

'That's why we've got to rescue the third Diamond,' said Katie seriously, 'so that all young creatures can enjoy the sea, without everything being spoiled by Mantora. Come on, we must go and solve that clue!'

The mermaids quickly said goodnight to their little playmate, while she was getting ready for bed. Ottilie deftly wrapped the long fronds of kelp round Lottie's soft tummy, like a woven blanket. This would stop the baby sea otter floating away in the night, as she slept on the gently rocking waves.

'That's so clever,' exclaimed Becky. She loved making things out of bits of seaweed and shells.

'Come on, Becky,' said the others, smiling. 'We haven't time to start weaving blankets from the kelp.'

'Quite right,' said Otto. 'It's time for your night mission! I'll show you around our shore. Stay close and quiet, in case of danger.' He started to swim away from the beds of kelp and towards the sandy bay. The mermaids rippled their tails to follow him.

'Take care that you don't swim near to any Human fishing boat returning home after a day's work,' whispered the father sea otter. He pointed with his black paw at the tall lighthouse ahead of them on the rocks. 'The lighthouse will soon be shining out to guide the boats home. We must look out for them.'

Looking around carefully, the mermaids swam through the warm waves until they reached the wide, lonely beach in front of the lighthouse rocks. The sand gleamed golden in the last rays of the sunset. Megan and the others pulled themselves out of the water and sat on the sand, facing the sea.

'So here we are at last, on the Golden Shore at night-time,' said Amber in a low voice. 'Has anyone got any ideas?'

'I think Poppy must be right that

the clue's "*Diamond in the night*" is
something to do with the stars,' said
Megan thoughtfully. 'Look how the stars
are reflected on the dark surface of the sea.
Perhaps the third Diamond is hidden
underneath one of those star reflections?'

'But which one?' wondered Amber.

'We'll just have to try and find out,'
urged Jess in a hurried whisper. 'We
haven't much time, so let's get to work.
*Mermaid SOS!*'

One by one, the mermaids slipped back
into the waves. Otto stayed on the sand to
keep guard. Wherever the young friends
saw a star's reflection shimmering on the
inky-blue surface of the sea, they dived
under it to search for the precious
Diamond. Their Stardust Lockets glowed

like lamps underneath the water, helping them to spot anything that might be useful or interesting.

'I've found a beautiful shell,' said Becky, as the mermaids hovered in the waves to examine their finds.

'I've found a piece of polished glass,' said Katie.

'And I've found an old boot!' exclaimed Poppy, holding it by the tips of her fingers and wrinkling her nose.

But there was no sign of the Snow Diamond. Megan sighed and looked up at the velvety sky.

'There are hundreds of stars shining now,' she said. 'I don't think we can search under the reflection of every single one.'

The mermaids bobbed about in the dark

sea, feeling very disheartened. Perhaps
Mantora had been right, and this clue
really would be impossible to solve. It was
a terrible thought.

Just at that moment, the friends saw a
beam of light sweeping across the surface
of the sea. It lit up a boat on the distant
horizon, then disappeared. A minute later,
the light swept round again.

'What's that?' asked Megan.

'It must be the light from the lighthouse,' replied Jess practically. 'Otto said it would shine out when the sky grew dark.'

Megan twisted round and looked up at the tall lighthouse, which stood on the rocks at the back of the beach. At the very top of it, an enormous lamp turned round and round, sending a powerful beam in every direction. In the darkness, the lamp looked like a huge eye, which blinked open and shut, open and shut…

She suddenly clapped her hands together and shouted joyfully to her friends, 'I've got it! I've solved the clue!'

# Chapter Five

'What do you mean, Megan?' asked the
mermaids in surprise.

'Look at the lighthouse lamp,' said
Megan excitedly. 'As it twists round, the
light seems to grow bigger. Then it seems
to grow smaller, as it turns away. It's just
like the clue – "*ever less and ever more*".
The Diamond shining in the night is the
lighthouse!'

'You're right,' said Poppy, with a rueful grin. 'I wish I'd thought of that.'

'How clever of you, Megan,' said Amber and the others.

'Hooray for Megan!' squeaked Sammy, blinking as he looked up at the rays of the lighthouse lamp.

Megan blushed with pleasure, happy to have helped her friends.

'But I still don't know exactly what to do next,' she confessed. 'The Snow Diamond must be near the lighthouse, but where exactly?'

Before the mermaids had time to think, they heard Otto splashing through the waves towards them.

'Duck down,' he hissed. 'Get beneath the waves! The Storm Gulls are heading this way again.'

With sinking hearts, the mermaids plunged underneath the surface of the sea. It seemed that the Storm Gulls would never leave them in peace. The young friends gathered in a circle round Otto, holding hands and staying as quiet as possible. One by one, the Storm Gulls swooped over the waves, then folded their dark wings and settled on the sea. They were just above the mermaids. Megan recognised the leader's harsh voice.

'There are rumours that the Sisters of the Sea are still hiding by the Golden Shore,' he croaked to the other Gulls. 'Although we have hunted here for them in vain, fear not, my brothers. They will never find what they are looking for. Not unless they can grow wings!'

'Ha, ha, haaaarrr!' laughed the Storm Gulls, jeering and screeching together.

'We'll leave them to their feeble plots and plans,' said the leader scornfully. 'Our Storm Queen,

Mantora, is waiting for us. Fly to her
swiftly.'

'*Swift as a storm*!' they all cried, setting
off with a flap and flurry of wings. Then
there was silence.

'Have they gone?' whispered Megan.

Otto splashed above the waves.

'It's all right,' he called. 'They are
already out of sight.'

The mermaids joined him thankfully,
puzzling over the words of the chief Storm
Gull.

'What did he mean, we need wings to
find the Diamond?' asked Becky.

'He was probably just being stupid,'
said Poppy crossly. 'Ooh, how I'd like to
peck him, the horrid mean thing!'

'No, Poppy,' said Megan thoughtfully. 'I

think he meant more than that.' She took
a deep breath and looked around. 'I think
the Storm Gulls have taken the Diamond
to the top of the lighthouse. And we'll
have to find it up there, somehow.'

The others followed her gaze in
astonishment. However would six young
mermaids get up to the top of the tall
lighthouse? They couldn't even get across
the beach to the rocks.

'B-b-but that really is impossible for us,'
stammered Amber.

'Oh no, it's not,'
smiled Katie. She
unhooked her
delicate Mermaid
Harp from its
plaited rope over her

shoulder. 'The Storm Gulls aren't the only creatures with wings.'

Strumming quickly, Katie played an urgent, dancing tune. The music rose into the still, dark night like a cry for help. Soon, the mermaids heard the soft beating of wings. Three, four, five, then six of the shearwaters they had seen earlier flew

across the bay. The sea birds swooped and circled over them.

'How can we help you, Sisters of the Sea?' they cried.

'Can you please fly to the top of the lighthouse?' pleaded Megan. 'See if you can find a precious Snow Diamond hidden up there. We must get it back, or Mantora will destroy our home in Ice Kingdom.'

The elegant birds soared away in the direction of the lighthouse. The mermaids watched them go, with hope growing in

their hearts. But all too soon, the shearwaters returned, shaking their heads sorrowfully. They settled on the bobbing waves in front of Megan and her friends.

'I am Sheldon,' said the biggest bird. 'There is something small and hard wedged into the window frame that shields the great light. It was too tightly stuck for us to pull it out with our beaks. Only the nimble fingers of a mermaid could release it.'

'But that means we'll have to get up to the top of the lighthouse ourselves!' exclaimed Jess. 'Oh, I do wish I could think of something.' She swished her tail impatiently, as she racked her brains for an idea.

'We must find a way,' urged Megan. 'If

we don't rescue the Diamond, we'll be letting everyone down. Not just Princess Arctica and our families, but all the young creatures of the sea.'

'Yes, like our friend Benjy the beluga whale,' said Amber.

'And the snow babies, Caspar and Max,' said Katie.

'And little Lottie,' added Megan sadly.

'Lottie!' cried Becky, with a snap of her fingers. 'That's it! Why didn't I think of that before? Come on, everyone, back to the kelp beds.'

With a flash of her peach-coloured tail,

Becky dived under the waves and set off towards the open sea.

'Wait! Becky!' her friends called, but she was already far ahead.

With a bewildered shrug of their shoulders, the others plunged after her. Sheldon and the shearwaters followed curiously, gliding through the air behind Otto and the mermaids. Soon they were all gathered round a very sleepy Lottie, who was wrapped up in her nest of kelp.

'Look,' explained Becky. 'Ottilie used the kelp to make a bed for Lottie. The long strands of seaweed are strong and flexible. They can't be easily broken. If we

make a woven mat from the kelp, the
shearwaters could carry one of us on it to
the top of the lighthouse!'

'You mean, like a flying carpet?'
breathed Megan, with shining eyes. 'What
a brilliant idea.'

'B-b-brilliant…' yawned Lottie sleepily.

Otto and Ottilie quickly showed the
mermaids how to gather the best strands
of kelp, and then Becky's clever fingers set
to work. The others helped her to weave
the long green and purple fronds together,
until they had made a strong, supple mat.
At each corner they left long, trailing ropes
for the sea birds to hold.

'There,' said Becky proudly. 'It's finished.
Now who is going to be brave enough to
fly on it, all the way up to the lighthouse?'

# Chapter Six

'I'd love to have a go,' said Jess daringly.
It was just the kind of adventure she would
enjoy. Then she noticed Megan looking
rather disappointed. Jess turned to her
friend with a flick of her turquoise tail.
'But I think you should be the one to do it,
Megan,' she added quickly. 'You worked
out that the Diamond was on top of the
lighthouse, after all. And you're so slight

and dainty that it will be easier for the
shearwaters to carry you.'

'Yes, Megan,' agreed the others, 'we
think you should go.'

'And I'll come with you,' said Sammy
importantly. 'Don't forget that we work as
a team!'

The mermaids held the woven mat aloft and swam with their friends to the edge of the shore, by the light of the moon. They spread their handiwork out on the sand, and Megan quickly wriggled on to it.

'Wait, Megan,' said Amber, as the shearwaters got ready to pull on the ropes. 'Take this little bag that our Inuit friend, Ana, gave to us. You might find it useful.'

Slowly, the birds flapped their strong wings and began to lift the little mat, and Megan, from the ground.

'Good luck! Hold tight!' called her friends, as she began to glide higher and higher through the air. The night breeze ruffled Megan's soft curls, and her tummy gave a funny lurch as she looked below her.

'We're so high up, Sammy,' she gasped.

'I hope we have made the mat strong enough.' She bravely held on tightly to the sides of the strange flying carpet, and looked ahead to the great lighthouse. Soon she was on a level with the big lamp, as it swung round behind its thick glass windows. The shearwaters hovered in the air, so that she could inspect the window frame.

'Close your eyes, Sammy, then the light won't dazzle you,' she whispered.

But when the light swung away, Megan gasped. Just as the shearwaters had said, there was a small bundle stuffed into a crack in the window frame.

'If only that really is the Diamond,' Megan murmured. She reached over precariously and tried to pull it out. 'It's stuck,' she puffed. 'I'll see if anything in Ana's bag might help.'

She quickly looked into the bag and lifted out Ana's carved knife. It had been

too small to cut the great blocks of frozen sea in Ice Kingdom, when the mermaids had rescued the beluga whales. But here it was just perfect for chipping away at the wooden window frame of the lighthouse.

Little by little, Megan worked until she had loosened the tantalising bundle, which

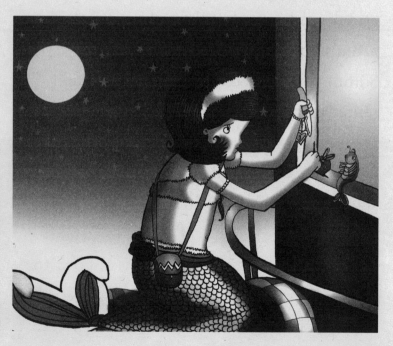

was wrapped up in thick seaweed. Then Sammy leaped lightly from the mat to the window frame. He pushed his body into the crack and heaved with all his might to release the seaweedy lump. The Stardust sprinkle that had fallen on the little Fairy Shrimp at the beginning of the adventures had given him extra, magical strength.

Sammy pushed and Megan pulled, Sammy pushed again and Megan pulled again, until…

'…I've got it!' said the brave young mermaid. 'Oh, Sheldon, let's fly quickly to show the others. Come on, Sammy, don't get left behind!'

Megan enjoyed the thrilling ride back to the sea, carried along gracefully by the friendly shearwaters. She looked down and

waved to her friends, hovering in the dark waves below her. Then the flying mat landed in the sea with a splash and Megan tumbled off into the water. All the mermaids were waiting for her, together with Otto, Ottilie and little Lottie.

'Lottie couldn't sleep,' explained her mother. 'She was so excited about you going to find the Diamond.'

'We don't know if I have found it yet,' said Megan shyly. 'We'll have to unwrap this bundle and see what's inside. Here, Lottie, why don't you do it?'

With huge, awestruck eyes, the baby sea otter helped to unwrap the layers of seaweed with her furry paws. Then she took something from the wrappings.

'That's so pretty!' she snuffled sleepily.

Everyone gasped when the third Snow Diamond dropped from Lottie's paw into Megan's hand.

'It's more than pretty, Lottie,' replied Megan solemnly, as she carefully showed them the glimmering Diamond. It sparkled white and yellow and purple. 'This will help to keep the world safe for all of us.'

'You've done well, Sisters of the Sea,' said Otto warmly. 'Princess Arctica will be proud of you.'

'We couldn't have done it without your help,' replied the mermaids. 'Or yours too, Sheldon.'

The birds flapped their wings proudly. 'We are only too happy to fight against Mantora and her evil Storm Gulls,' they cried. 'But see! The dawn is glowing pink and gold in the east. It is time for us to fly on. Goodbye!'

'Goodbye!' called Megan. 'Thank you!'

'And we must go back to our home in the kelp,' said Otto. 'Lottie can hardly stop yawning after this excitement. But don't forget us, Mermaids. And you too, Sammy! Remember

that the sea otters of the Golden Shore will always be your grateful friends.'

Otto and his family swam away, humming the old Mermaid tune in their wild, playful voices:

*'You've seen the otters*
*Swim and play,*
*So don't forget*
*This golden day...'*

As the sea otters disappeared from view, Katie said, 'Isn't it marvellous that we've found the Diamond?'

'And isn't it marvellous that we have made so many new friends on our quest?' replied Megan, as she tucked the Diamond into her gleaming Stardust Locket. 'But we are still only half-way through our task. We can't celebrate yet.'

For a moment, the mermaids fell silent, swirling their tails in the waves, as the morning sun rose in the sky. They were thinking about Princess Arctica and their families, waiting anxiously for them to return Ice Kingdom with all six Snow Diamonds. And time was running out...

'Is there a message from Mantora with your Diamond, Megan?' asked Jess, breaking the silence. Megan quickly looked through the discarded seaweed wrappings. A lurid orange scroll was hidden amongst them. She lifted it out, and then looked around with large, solemn eyes.

'Here you are, Jess,' she said, handing the scroll to her friend. 'This must be the fourth clue.'

The mermaids looked at one another in wonder. They really had solved the first

three clues! What would be in the next one? And would it be even trickier than the third clue had been? Jess took a deep breath, and slowly began to unroll the fateful scroll...

Whatever it said, and wherever it sent them, the Sisters of the Sea were sure of one thing. Working out the fourth clue would be their biggest challenge yet – and they had to solve it soon, before it was too late!

Amber has golden curls and a gleaming lilac tail. She looks after her friends, and is a good leader.

Katie enjoys playing her Mermaid Harp. She has a long plait over her shoulder and a sparkly lemon-coloured tail.

Megan has sweet wavy hair and a spangled pink and white tail. She is never far from her pet Fairy Shrimp, Sammy.

Jess is bold and brave, with dark curls and a dazzling turquoise tail. She is friends with Monty, the humpback whale.

Becky loves the beauty of the sea. Her hair is decorated with flowers, and her tail is a pretty peach colour.

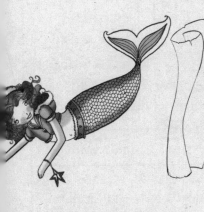

Poppy has coppery curls, a bright blue tail, and bags of confidence, but her impatience can land her in trouble.